The Case of the Stuck Truck

By Cecilia Minden

TJ and Mark like to help.

Russ likes trucks.

4

Oh no! His truck is stuck!

His truck is stuck in the sand.

6 Russ pulls on his truck.

Russ cannot pull up his truck.

TJ digs in the sand.

The truck is still stuck.

Mark digs under the truck.

The truck is still stuck.

TJ and Mark pull on the truck.
They pull up the truck!

Good work, TJ.
Good work, Mark.

Word List

sight words

and	His	Mark	They	work
cannot	is	no	TJ	
Good	like	oh	to	
help	likes	the	under	

short a words	short i words	short o words	short u words	
sand	digs	on	pull	truck
	in		pulls	trucks
	still		Russ	up
			stuck	

14

TJ and Mark like to help.
Russ likes trucks.
Oh no! His truck is stuck!
His truck is stuck in the sand.
Russ pulls on his truck.
Russ cannot pull up his truck.
TJ digs in the sand.
The truck is still stuck.
Mark digs under the truck.

The truck is still stuck.
TJ and Mark pull on the truck.
They pull up the truck!
Good work, TJ. Good work, Mark.

Published in the United States of America by Cherry Lake Publishing
Ann Arbor, Michigan
www.cherrylakepublishing.com

Illustrator: Becky Down

Cherry Blossom Press is an imprint of Cherry Lake Publishing.

Library of Congress Cataloging-in-Publication Data

Names: Minden, Cecilia, author. | Down, Becky, illustrator.
Title: The case of the stuck truck / written by: Cecilia Minden ; illustrated by Becky Down.
Description: [Ann Arbor : Cherry Lake Publishing, 2019] | Series: Little blossom stories |
    Summary: "Help TJ and Mark solve the case of the stuck truck!"– Provided by publisher. |
    Includes author biography, phonetics, and teaching guide.
Identifiers: LCCN 2019006061| ISBN 9781534149748 (pbk.) |
    ISBN 9781534148314 (pdf) | ISBN 9781534151178 (hosted ebook)
Subjects: | CYAC: Mystery and detective stories.
Classification: LCC PZ7.M6539 Cbs 2019 | DDC [E]–dc23
LC record available at https://lccn.loc.gov/2019006061

Printed in the United States of America
Corporate Graphics

Cecilia Minden is the former director of the Language and Literacy Program at Harvard Graduate School of Education. She earned her PhD in Reading Education at the University of Virginia. Dr. Minden has written extensively for early readers. She is passionate about matching children to the very book they need to improve their skills and progress to a deeper understanding of all the wonder books can hold. Dr. Minden and her family live in McKinney, Texas.